T0113336

Hard Times
in the
Valley *of* Korah

WILL GOD SAVE
THE EMELLIAN BIRDS OR
ZION THE WORM?

Author and Illustrator

Bertha Ramsey

WESTBOW
PRESS®
A DIVISION OF THOMAS NELSON
& ZONDERVAN

WestBow Press books may be ordered through booksellers or by contacting:

WestBow Press
A Division of Thomas Nelson & Zondervan
1663 Liberty Drive
Bloomington, IN 47403
www.westbowpress.com
1 (866) 928-1240

ISBN: 978-1-5127-5647-0 (sc)
ISBN: 978-1-5127-5648-7 (e)

Library of Congress Control Number: 2016915013

Print information available on the last page.

WestBow Press rev. date: 11/09/2016

It's the beginning of summer. The birds and worms have plenty to eat and drink. They are happy. They've never dealt with much hardship, except for the death of a love one. There are plenty of insects, worms, and seed available for the birds to eat. There is plenty of water and moist soil for the worms. They are living in a land God would call "a land that flows with milk and honey." God has supplied their needs bountifully down through the generations. However, something will happen that has never happened to any of them.

As summer gets hotter, the number of rainy days decrease to once a week. The inhabitants of this land are accustomed to heavy rain two to three times weekly. The birds and worms still have plenty of food and water. They began to see a small decrease in resources. Nobody feels the need to pray to God about such a small matter.

Nanny Bell, the eldest of the Emellian (E-mel-li-an) Bird family, has had her own share of hard times. But she is not prepared for what will happen in the Valley of Korah.

Midsummer sets in. The birds and worms notice a great decrease in their food and water supply. The heat is almost unbearable, depleting most plants of moisture. The temperature fluctuates each day, sometimes ninety degrees and higher. During the night the moon shines. A slight wind blows, cooling the air between 68 to 72 degrees. The dew has stopped giving the grasses their nightly watering. The birds, worms, and other inhabitants began to notice that there are no clouds forming in the sky to give rain or shade. God told the clouds to stay away until he needed them.

It hasn't rain for two weeks. The ground has formed cracks. Most of the worms, bugs, and other insects have gone into the cracks to find water and get food from plant roots. The birds are finding it hard to survive without their usual meals of worms, insects, and plant seed. Still, no one calls on God.

There is a family of birds called the Emellians [E-mel-li-ans]. The birds reside on Mato [May-toe] Hill in the Valley of Korah. They live in large nests built of straw and twigs. The nests are located on the ground under huge oak trees. Each couple has their own nest. Nanny Bell shares her nest with the chicks.

Leeli and Dan are finding it hard to feed the family no matter how early they awake and hunt. Other birds in the valley also look for food, making it difficult to find enough for all. Nanny Bell hates to see her family worry. She's never had to face these hard times before. Unsure of what to do, she knows something has to be done. She has to be strong for her family.

However, she comes up with the best solution possible. "Two weeks have gone by with no rain," Nanny Bell tells her family, "We hardly have food." She knows their only hope is if her sons search away from the valley. But then she risks never seeing them again. Her husband, Ed, left the valley years ago to get something special for her birthday and never returned. She continues to pray for his return. She refuses to believe Ed is dead. Without food, they will not survive. It's up to her sons to find some.

"Unfortunately, food is a scarce commodity to us all on Mato Hill and throughout the entire valley." Therefore, she tells her sons to search for food and be careful.

The eldest son, Leeli, tries to ease Nanny Bell's mind by saying, "We will be okay." He says good-bye to his wife, Josey, and daughter, Sally Sue. Likewise, Dan says good-bye to his wife, Ava, and daughter, Hanna. They all hug one another.

Leeli tells the family that they don't need to worry and that they will return with plenty. However, fear is lurking in his mind. Leeli remembers his dad telling him while he was yet a small chick, "I'll return soon. I'm leaving the valley to search for a special birthday gift for your mom. Be a good little chick for me!" Till this very day, he still wonders about the disappearance of his dad.

Leeli and Dan have never left the valley. The chicks do not want their dads to leave home. They are too young to understand why their dads are leaving. The family wishes them well. They pray together before the sons set off. The brothers hate the idea of leaving their family behind, and hope the family can salvage something from the grasses until they return. They grab their packs and set off. They only took drinking water to prevent dehydration. The Emellian Birds are not good flyers. Walking is their main way of travel.

Days go by. It's been three weeks, and there's still no rain. The ground continues to crack open. Water is in short supply. Dan and Leeli have been gone seven days now. Only the roots of small edible plants remain alive now. Josey and Ava search through the dead grass for food. Sometimes the family goes one or two days without eating. But today they are blessed and find something to eat.

Sally Sue knows she should not complain about the food shortage. She also knows she doesn't feel well and has to tell someone. So she tells Nanny Bell. "Nanny Bell, my tummy hurts," she cries. Nanny Bell eyes began to fill with water as the chick tells of her stomach pain. Nanny Bell knows these are hunger pains. There are still no sign of her sons coming with food. She fights back the tears to keep them from falling. She doesn't want the chicks to see her cry. She has to be strong at a time like this.

"Come over, Sally Sue," she says. The little one comes over to her. She begins to rub Sally Sue's tummy as if she's trying to rub the hunger away. Sally Sue falls asleep. The rubbing has eased her pain for now.

The clouds ask God to allow them to return over the valley. God replies, "Not now! I see them. I must allow them to endure hardship sometimes. I have always given them plenty. They have forgotten me. For this reason, I cannot allow you to return over the valley. I want them to call for me and trust me."

Josey asks her mother-in-law, Nanny Bell, if Sally Sue is okay. She tells her that the chick is suffering from hunger pains. Josey tells Ava about the situation at hand and asks if Hanna has complained of having any pains. "No," Ava answers, "but I noticed yesterday she was rubbing her tummy. She's asleep now. She's okay, I guess." Ava cries to Josey, "We have to do something!"

"Calm down," said Josey. "We don't want to wake the girls."

"I wonder if our husbands are okay. I've seen Nanny Bell watching for them from the treetop," Ava says. Now, Josey wonders the same thing. She looks over at her daughter. "I can't allow my mind to go there. I have to think positive thoughts." Ava is afraid and fears the worse. She looks over at Hanna. She remains asleep. "Positive thoughts it is," she replies as tears trickles down her face.

Early the next morning before sunrise, the wives tell Nanny Bell they will hunt early for food before the chicks wake. Ava smiles. "What are you smiling about?" Josey asks.

Ava replies, "I was just wondering if hunting early will we get the worm." Josey and Nanny Bell laugh. It's the first time they have laughed in weeks. All of the birds in the Valley of Korah are searching of the same thing—food.

They leave home early. While on the hunt, they find three dead bugs. They gather the bugs and take them home. A pact is made. They decide to split whatever they find five ways. That way they will all survive another day together. The Emellian family thanks God for the three bugs and eats them. God notices the most remarkable thing. The birds thank him for their meal. His plan is working. In the meantime He continues to watch them.

Underground, there lives a worm by the name of Zion. He is young, alone, and very thirsty. He lives approximately one foot underground. The moist soil is at least three feet lower. The other day when he felt he didn't have the strength to tunnel that deep, he decided to reside within that first foot of soil. Plant roots were keeping it moist then, but they are now depleted of any moisture. He has never heard of these conditions in the valley.

Zion gets water through eating moist soil. He knows he needs to find some fast. The heat from the sun had already dried up the uncovered parts of the ground. Zion thinks, *If I could just find a huge rock to crawl under, I know there will be enough moisture under it so that I can eat and live.* Zion tries to eat through the hard, dry ground. He knows his life depends on it. "I am a young worm! I have not lived life to the fullest! I have dreams! I don't have a wife or children!" he cries aloud to God.

It's now been three and a half weeks with no rain or dew. Zion lifts his head above ground to see if a huge rock is near. Suddenly, a familiar smell enters his nose. It's the smell of moist soil. He looks toward the direction of the smell, and he notices the huge rock. His first thought is, *Should I crawl on top of the ground?* His second thought is, *The heat from the sun will probably destroy me.* Finally, he makes a decision to continue tunneling underground.

After a while he becomes tired. The smell of moist soil motivates him to keep going. He wants a wife and children more than anything. Zion knows that the only way he can have them is by staying alive. Therefore, he prays to God to allow him to make it to the huge rock safely. He also asks God to protect him from all hurt, harm, and danger while on his journey.

The next day the chicks are hungry again. They rub their tummies. Nanny Bell takes them to the larger water hole, where all of the birds of the Valley of Korah now drink. The small water hole near their home has dried. The large water hole is drying out as well. It has enough water for another week or so. They drink. Their tummies feel better, though the chicks remain hungry.

Sally Sue begins to question Nanny Bell about the situation at hand. She doesn't have answers. They have never experienced a drought or famine before. They begin to pray to God for food. "Please, God! Please send us food, or else we die."

Then Nanny Bell cries aloud, "Lord, send the rain! Lord, help us!"

Again, the clouds ask God to allow them to give rain to the valley. God replies, "Not yet!"

Zion begins to tire again. Coincidently, he isn't far away from the rock. He's approximately two feet away from it. Tunneling through the hard soil feels like it's taking forever, and it's drained much-needed strength from him. So he decides to come out of the ground to determine his distance from the huge rock. The smell of the moist soil is very strong now. It's so strong he can taste it. At this very moment, he feels glee and hope. "Thank you, Lord. I'm saved," he prays silently. Though strong in spirit, he remains physically weak. "I can't give up now," he murmurs to himself. God continues to watch and listen.

Zion is not aware of his surroundings he's coming out of the ground. He's just relieved to be out. He thinks, *I'll just rest for a minute or so. That way the heat will not destroy me.* "Help me, Lord. I want to live!" he cries.

The birds have just finished praying to God for food. They look on the ground. Surprisingly, Zion is on the ground in plain sight. It just so happens that he chewed his tunnel exit in the very midst of the hungry birds. Zion looks plump to the birds. The birds gaze upon Zion. Finally, he looks up. To his surprise, he is staring in the faces of danger. He can no longer move fast enough to get away, even though his exit hole is right behind him.

The birds are very hungry, and they had just prayed to God to send them food. The Emellian family believe that God has answered their prayers. However, they don't know that Zion has also prayed to God to protect him from all hurt, harm, and danger. Josey reminds the family of the pact they all made together. "That way, we may all eat and live to see another day together."

Sally Sue looks at the worm. She is hungry. But for some strange reason, she feels sadness. Just the thought of eating him makes her feel regretful. The others have the look of curiosity on their faces. *Why is Sally Sue crying after seeing the worm?* Zion is still dazed and fears his life is in danger. He wonders, *God, did you hear my prayer?*

Then Josey whispers to Sally Sue, "God answered our prayers. We need to eat this worm so that we may live."

Nanny Bell tells her, "We prayed to God just now for this food. You prayed with us too. What's wrong, child? Why do you not want to eat this worm? Before the famine, you had no problem eating worms."

"What if he's the last worm living in Mato Hill or the entire Valley of Korah?" Sally Sue asks.

Josey assures her daughter that he's not. "The other worms are deep within the ground, living in the cracks and tunnels, awaiting rain, and surviving on what foods and water they find in plant roots." Sally Sue feels comfort, knowing that Zion is not the last worm. She is hungry, and she now wants to eat to sustain her life. Nanny Bell laughs. "Thank you, God, for this worm." Then she says out loud, "Let's eat!"

Zion looks at the birds and reflects on his life. The birds don't know it yet, but Leeli and Dan are approaching Mato Hill. What will happen to Zion? Will God answer Zion's prayers to protect him from all hurt, harm, and danger and let him live? Will the Emellian Bird family eat him? Is it possible that Leeli and Dan have brought food for the family? Will Zion escape?

Zion knows he's not far from the exit hole of his tunnel. He figures if he maneuvers himself backward slowly toward the hole, there's a chance he could escape. He is the first live prey the birds have seen in a week. Josey and Ava have no intentions of letting the chicks cry themselves to sleep from hunger tonight. The birds need food. Zion needs water. Zion knows he's only about two feet away from the huge rock.

The rock is located on the opposite side of the birds. He is stuffed and can't eat anymore soil. He knows his chances of survival are slim if he doesn't obtain water soon. The heat from the sun is starting to warm his body. Zion cries. "Help me, Lord! Help me Lord!" He can't understand the birds. The birds can't understand him. The birds are saying, "Thank you, Lord! Thank you, Lord! Thank you for this worm."

Suddenly, Leeli and Dan arrive home. As they top Mato Hill, Sally Sue is the first to see them. She screams, "Papa, Papa!" Everyone looks about to see what the excitement is all about. The wives and chicks run to greet and welcome them home. Nanny Bell walks at a slow pace, thanking God that her sons have returned. In all the excitement, no one has noticed that Leeli and Dan have brought home a very special and long-awaited surprise.

Zion realizes he has a chance to escape, and he does. Slowly, he crawls toward the huge rock, praying and watching the birds the whole time. Finally, he reaches the huge rock. He thanks God, "I didn't get eaten by the birds. You protected me. Thank you, Lord!"

Leeli and Dan brought enough food to feed the family for a while. Their packs are filled with nuts, berries, seeds, and insects. The family is happy once again. Nanny Bell approaches her sons. "I thank God the two of you made it home safe. I've been so worried about you," she says.

"Glad to see you too," her sons reply. Dan hugs his mom. Then she turns to Leeli and hugs him. Heavy tears run down Nanny Bell's cheeks and cloud her vision. "I'm so happy. God has returned you to me."

Leeli and Dan purposely do not tell the family that Papa Ed will soon arrive on the hill. Then Hanna sees a shadow growing taller and taller, creeping up the hill. She then alerts Sally Sue, who is busy admiring her dad. "Sally Sue!" she yells. "Come quick! Someone is coming!" Sally Sue watches as the shadow grows closer, and then she alerts the family. "Someone is coming! Someone is coming!"

The family looks on in amazement with beaks wide open. The wives cling to their husbands as if afraid of the unknown. Everyone focuses on the slow-moving shadow. Leeli and Dan stand tall with smiles on their faces, not saying a word, just watching the shadow along with everyone else. Finally, they see a body. It's Papa Ed. He has returned home to the Valley of Korah on Mato Hill. His sons found home in a distant valley, going through his own share of hard times. They rescued him. Papa Ed rejoices that deliverance came after twenty years. Josey, Ava, and the chicks have no earthly idea about the stranger standing before them. The sons keep silent.

Nanny Bell's beak closes so tight she can hardly swallow. Her wings flop down at her side. She focuses her vision on the elder bird. She looks him over. She is speechless. She can't move. Papa Ed sees Nanny Bell, the woman of his dreams for many, many years. He has never forgotten her. His beak closes so tight he can hardly swallow. His wings flop down at his sides. He focuses all of his attention on her. He is speechless. He can't move either. No one interferes. They watch the two, wondering what will happen next.

Then Papa Ed screams, "Bell! Oh, my sweet Bell. I have missed you so much." He swings his wings around her and hugs her so tight, not letting go. She's still speechless and motionless, her eyes wide. After a while she lets go of a loud cry and lays her head against his chest. In shock, she remains unable to utter words. She just cries. Josey asks in a soft tone, "Who is he?"

Leeli replies, "Our dad. Family, this is Papa Ed. This is the man Nanny Bell spoke so much about and prayed day after day for his return home." Joy bells ring in the hearts of the entire Emellian Bird family on that day. They feast, give thanks to God, and enjoy one another. Papa Ed reaches under his wing and gives Bell the gift he found for her twenty years ago before his dilemma began. He gives her a beautiful, sparkling garnet stone that he'd carved into the shape of a cross. He made a necklace for her with it. "It was for your birthday twenty years ago. It was just a stone. When I had time, I carved it into a cross just for you. I had hopes of giving it to you someday. I feel today is as good a time as any to finally give it to you," he says as tears fill his eyes.

Zion, on the other hand, crawls under the huge rock for refuge. He ate his share of moist soil. Now feeling better, he begins to thank God for delivering him. He also thanks God for protecting him from all hurt, harm, and danger along the way. "God delivered," is his last comment as the tired worm drifts off to sleep.

The next day Zion regains his strength. He feels better, and he is no longer dazed. He can see clearly. After getting his fill of moist soil again, he begins tunneling downward. He tunnels down a foot or so. To his surprise, he tunnels right into the dwelling place of his brother, Kenny Worm. They are thrilled to see each other. He is introduced to Kenny's wife, Sandraiah (San-dray-ah). She introduces him to her friend, Traci, who is also in the dwelling place. Traci is the most beautiful female worm he has ever seen. For him, it's love at first sight. Traci feels the same exact way. Zion begins to thank God within his mind, "Lord, you heard my cry. You listened to me. Thank you, Lord. All of my hopes and dreams are beginning to come to pass." Zion and Traci become husband and wife the very next day. What a happy day for the Worm family.

God is well pleased with everything He has seen and heard over the past several weeks. God makes a final decision. He calls the clouds. He tells them to cover the entire Valley of Korah and give them rain. The clouds rejoice. They begin to send rain, slow at first and then heavy—and slow to heavy for the next three days. The Bird and Worm families began to thank and praise God for giving them the rain and sustaining their lives. God is pleased.

The valley is returning to normal. Insects roam freely. Grass is growing. Ponds are filled. Papa Ed is developing a relationship with his family. Zion and Traci start a new beginning together. Sometimes your answered prayer may come in twenty years, a month, a day, or whatever God's will is for your life. Just hang in there. Endure the hard times, and believe God is with you and watching over you. Don't forget he wants your praises throughout your waiting.

Special Thanks

Reslyn Ramsey, my daughter

Shawn Ramsey, my son

Kenda Ormond, my cousin

Sharvaysha Reed, guardian daughter

Mary Bennamon

Brittany Bennamon

Clara White

Malikah Jones

Ruby Rankins

Sabrina and others

Greatest Appreciation

Thank you, WestBow Press, for publishing my first book. Thank you for your patience and guidance every step of the way.

Thanks always to God!

How the Story Began

I had some spare time on my hands one night in September 2015. So I took out a sheet of plain white paper. I began to doddle. What started out as a bowling pin soon took the form of five birds and a worm. From there, a story was born.

Printed in the United States
By Bookmasters